SURPRISE!

For Hannah
Thanks to David and Matt

Quarto is the authority on a wide range of topics.

Quarto educates, entertains and enriches the lives of
our readers—enthusiasts and lovers of hands-on living.

www.quartoknows.com

Copyright © words & pictures 2017

First published in 2017 by

words & pictures, Part of The Quarto Group,

6 Orchard, Lake Forest, CA 92630

A CIP record for the book is available from the Library of Congress.

ISBN: 978 1 91027 741 6

1 3 5 7 9 8 6 4 2

Printed in China

SURPRISE!

Mike Henson

words & pictures

"SSSShh!"

"Huh?"

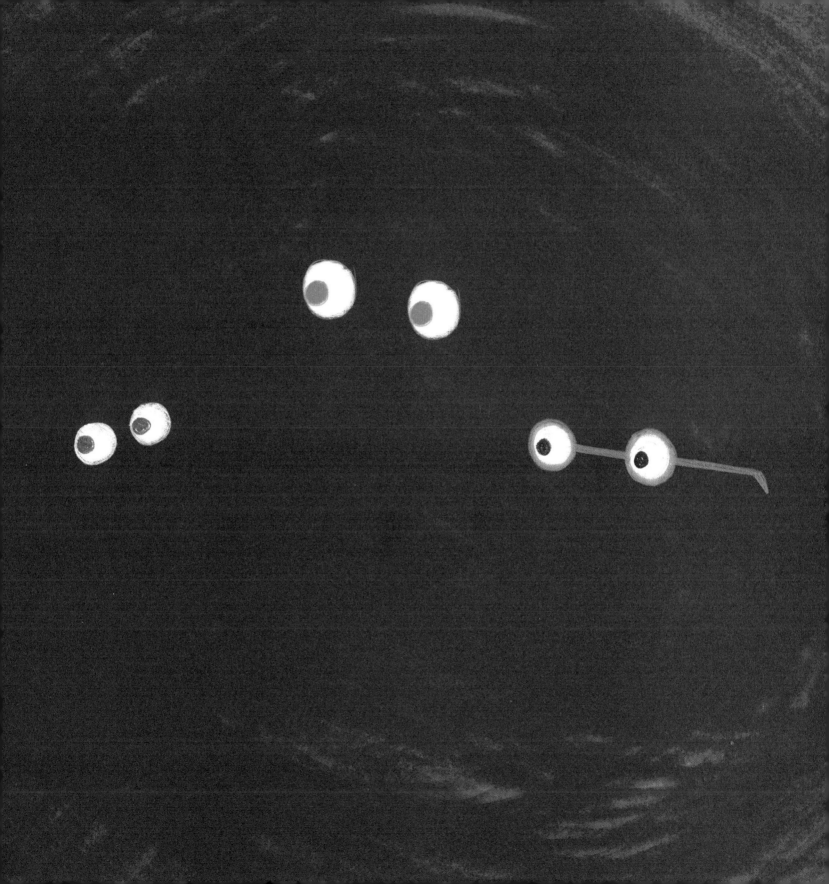

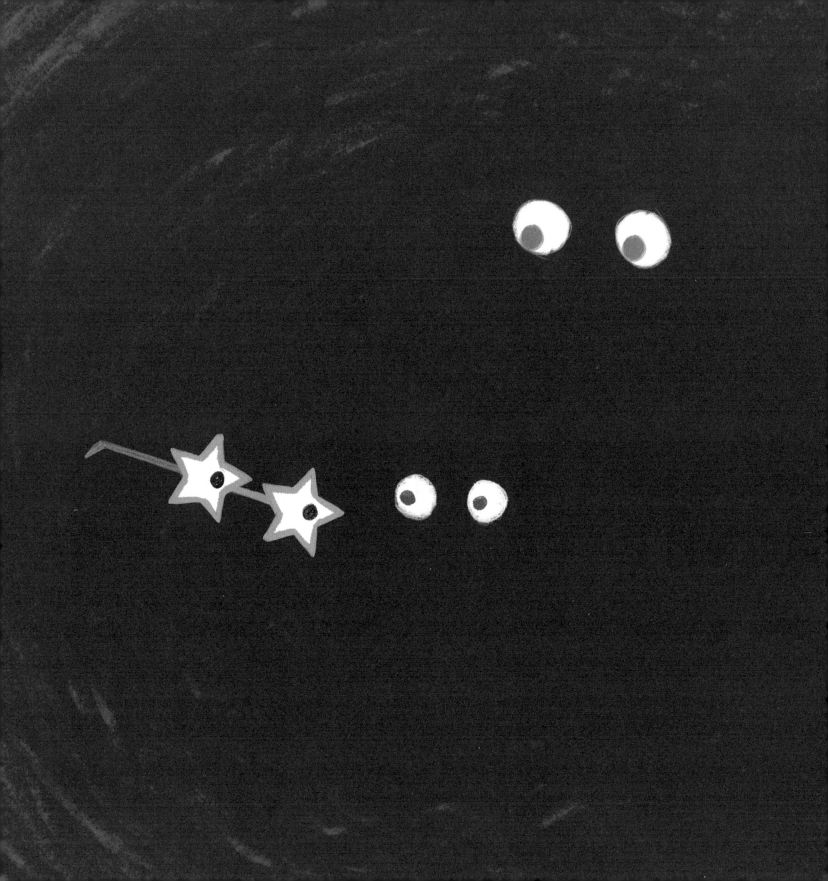

"Surprise!"

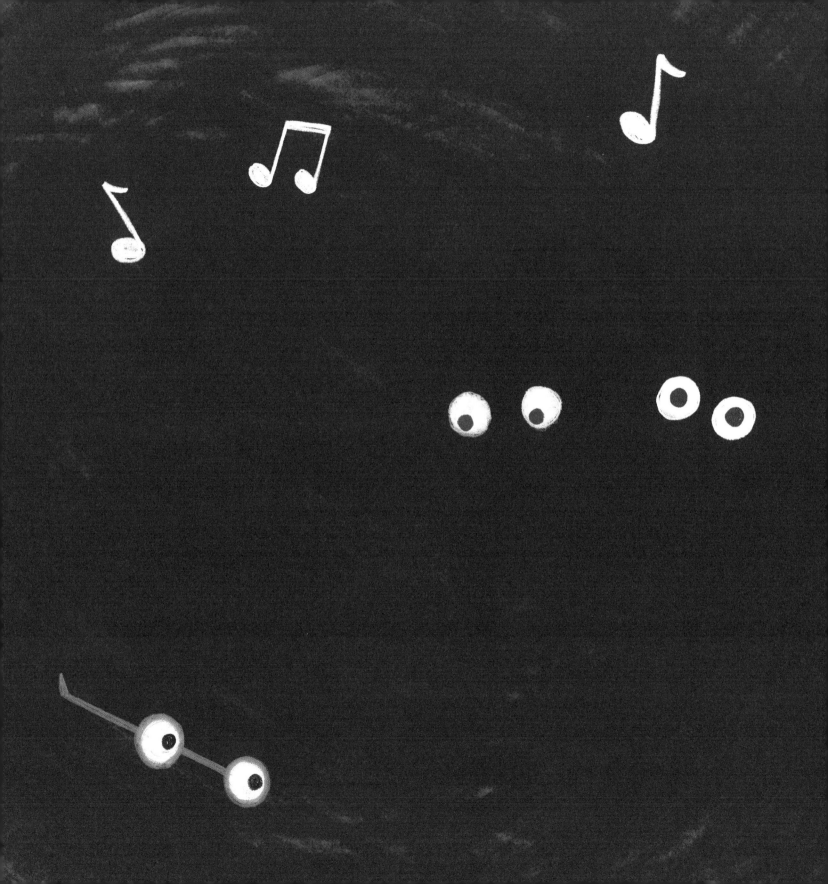

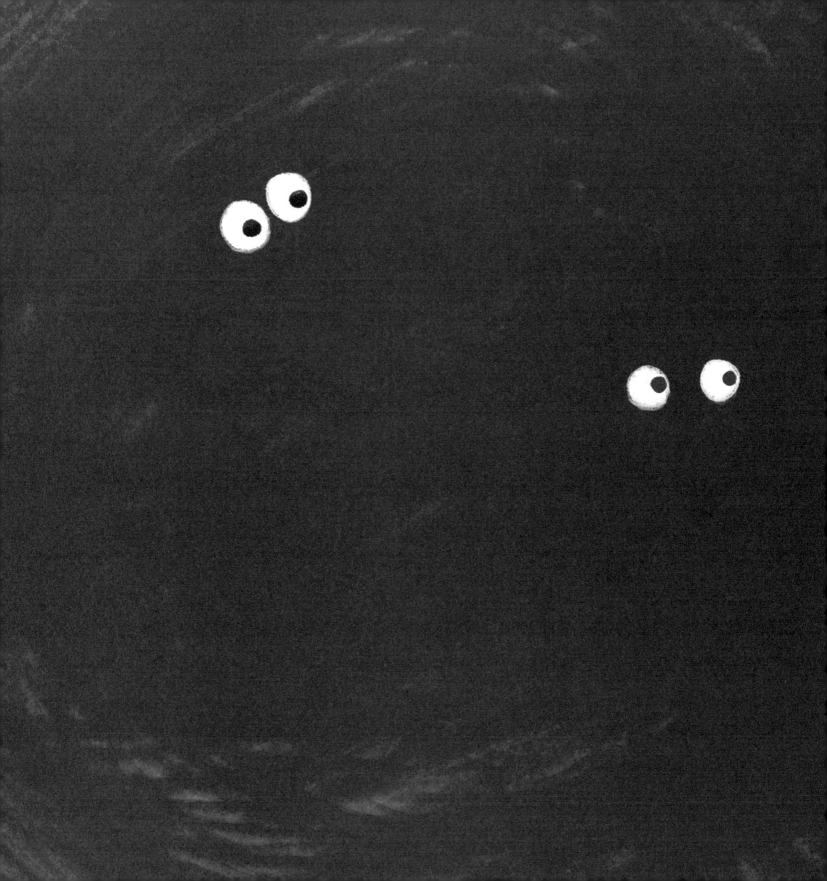

"Surprise!"

"Oh my!
This party
is amazing!"

"Every time
the light goes on,
there's a fantastic ..."

"Huh?"

"Oooh!"